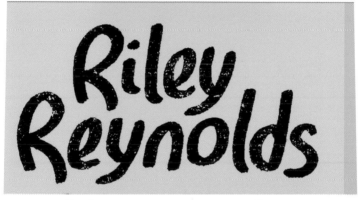

ROCKS THE PARK

created by

JAY ALBEE

STONE ARCH BOOKS
a capstone imprint

Published by Stone Arch Books, an imprint of Capstone
1710 Roe Crest Drive, North Mankato, Minnesota 56003
capstonepub.com

Library of Congress Cataloging-in-Publication Data
Title: Riley Reynolds rocks the park / written and illustrated by Jay Albee.
Description: North Mankato, Minnesota : Stone Arch Books, 2022. | Series:
Riley Reynolds | Audience: Ages 7-10. | Audience: Grades 2-3. |
Summary: Nonbinary fourth grader Riley and their friends learn how
small, simple parks can be just as important and fun as fancy new parks.
Identifiers: LCCN 2021058801 (print) | LCCN 2021058802 (ebook) | ISBN
9781666344059 (hardcover) | ISBN 9781666344097 (paperback) | ISBN
9781666344134 (pdf) Subjects: LCSH: Gender nonconformity—Juvenile
fiction. | Urban parks—Pennsylvania—Philadelphia—Juvenile fiction. |
Friendship—Juvenile fiction. | South Philadelphia (Philadelphia, Pa.)—Juvenile
fiction. | CYAC: Parks—Fiction. | City and town life—Fiction. | Friendship—
Fiction. | Gender identity—Fiction. | LCGFT: Fiction. Classification: LCC
PZ7.1.A4294 Ril 2022 (print) | LCC PZ7.1.A4294 (ebook) | DDC 813.6 (Fic)—
dc23/eng/20211223
LC record available at https://lccn.loc.gov/2021058801
LC ebook record available at https://lccn.loc.gov/2021058802

Special thanks to Manu Shadow Velasco for their consultation.

Designed by Nathan Gassman
Printed and bound in the USA. 4882

TABLE OF CONTENTS

I'M RILEY!

I LOVE SO MANY THINGS! I LOVE CRAFTING.

THE ONLY THING BETTER THAN MAKING MESSES IS MAKING COOL STUFF.

MX. AUDE TEACHES HELPFUL TERMS

Cisgender: Cisgender (or cis) people identify with the gender written on their birth certificate. They are usually boys or girls.

Gender identity: Regardless of the gender written on a person's birth certificate, they decide their gender identity. It might change over time. A person's interests, clothes, and behavior might be traditionally associated with their gender identity, or they might not.

Honorific: Young people use honorifics when they talk to or about adults, especially teachers. Mr. is the honorific for a man, Mrs. or Ms. for a woman, and Mx. is the gender-neutral honorific often used for nonbinary people. It is pronounced "mix." Nonbinary people may also use Mr., Mrs., or Ms. as well.

LGBTQ+: This stands for lesbian, gay, bisexual (also pansexual), transgender, queer. There are lots of ways people describe their gender and attraction. These are just a few of those ways. The + sign means that there are many, many more, and they are all included in the acronym LGBTQ+.

Nonbinary: Nonbinary people have a gender identity other than boy or girl. They may be neither, both, a combination, or sometimes one and sometimes the other.

Pronouns: Pronouns are how people refer to themselves and others (she/her, they/them, he/him, etc.). Pronouns often line up with gender identity (especially for cis people), but not always. It's best to ask a person what pronouns they like to use.

Queer: An umbrella term for people who identify as LGBTQ+.

Transgender: Transgender (or trans) people do not identify with the gender listed on their birth certificate. They might identify as the other binary gender, both genders, or another gender identity.

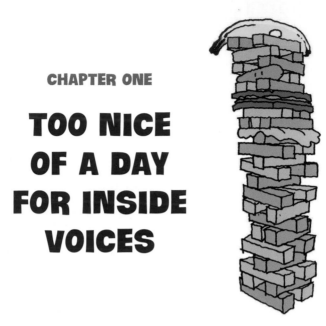

CHAPTER ONE

TOO NICE OF A DAY FOR INSIDE VOICES

The Jenga tower was tall. Maybe the tallest one Riley and their friends had ever built. The tower was wobbly too. It would fall at any moment. It didn't help that they had added parts of their lunch to it—a lettuce leaf, a baby carrot, an apple slice, a bit of cheddar, a whole PB&J, and even a banana.

It was Riley's turn. They walked around the tower, which was stacked on the kitchen table. They took it in from every side. Lea trembled as much as the tower with anticipation. Cricket did the robot computer voice he did when he was excited.

"*Beep-boop-boop-beep.* Chance of falling ninety-eight percent!"

"Ha!" scoffed Riley. "Not if I can help it!"

Riley tapped one block. Then another. Then the first one again. They gently pushed the block—and it came out! The tower wobbled! Riley held their breath, Lea squealed, and Cricket gasped.

Riley climbed onto a kitchen chair and slowly placed the block on top of the tower. It wobbled!

It tipped!

It fell!

The friends shouted and squealed and beeped and booped with delight as the blocks tumbled.

"Did you see that?" shouted Riley. "I nearly had it!"

"Ha!" shouted Lea. "Not even!"

"Statistically very unlikely!" shouted Cricket. The bottom third of the tower stayed standing. Lea swiped at it just before Riley could. Those blocks went clattering too. The three friends whooped and hollered.

Riley's dad came into the kitchen wearing his painting clothes. "That sounded like a big one! Who won?"

"Not me," said Riley, smiling wide.

Riley liked winning Jenga but losing when the tower was super tall was just as good.

"Uh-oh, Dad. You've got deadline hair."

When Dad was working on a painting, he wore his long hair in a scrunchie that Riley gave him. But when he was on a deadline, his hair just wouldn't stay tied back.

When Dad was stressed out, he forgot things twice as much. He paced up and down and sometimes got worried that his paintings were no good. But mostly he scratched his head, and ran his fingers through his hair, and tugged at it in big handfuls.

"The hair doesn't lie! This painting is due today and I'm starting to worry

I won't get it finished in time." Dad saw a pile of tote bags in the corner of the room. "Oh no! I forgot! When Mama got called into work this morning, she asked if we could run those things to Toby around the corner."

"We could do it," said Riley. Jenga was fun, but they'd been playing for a while. It was a nice day, and Riley liked Toby. And besides, Dad needed to focus on his painting.

"Sure thing," agreed Cricket and Lea.

"Thanks, kids. That'll really help me out. Mama too," said Dad. Dad let out a deep breath. His hair calmed down a little too.

"Maybe we'll stop at the park on the way back," said Riley.

"Sounds good," said Dad. "I'll meet you there later. Message if you leave for somewhere else."

"Got it, Dad," said Riley. Riley, Cricket, and Lea loaded up with tote bags to take to Toby.

"Thanks, Ry. Be safe!" said Dad.

As they walked out the door, Riley thought Dad's hair was definitely de-frazzled a little. Riley was glad.

CHAPTER TWO

TOBY AND THE WILDER STREET PARK

Riley, Lea, and Cricket stomped down Riley's stoop carrying the heavy tote bags.

"Why are we bringing bags of dirt to Toby?" asked Cricket.

"Not dirt," said Riley, "daffodil bulbs. They're like big seeds. Mama and I just pulled them up from our plot in the community garden. Mama wants to plant more tomatoes. Tomatoes are fine, but I wish the whole plot was daffodils. I wanted to keep these and give Toby the tomatoes instead."

"These will make a lot of flowers," said Lea.

"Especially since they're magical," said Cricket. "They multiply when you water them after midnight."

"Cool," smiled Lea. "We could make heaps and sell them!"

"We can't," said Cricket. "They'd grow into a beanstalk with a giant at the top. These are the same plants as from that one story."

Lea rolled her eyes. "Those were magic beans."

"What if they were daffodil beans?" said Riley. "Don't accidentally eat one, okay. One of my cousins did that once and daffodils grew out of her ears."

Lea didn't quite believe Riley, but she had to be sure. "Which cousin?" she asked.

"Angelica," replied Riley quickly.

"Angelica doesn't have daffodils growing out of her ears!" said Lea.

"Of course not," said Cricket. "She trims them every day."

The bags were heavy, but it wasn't far to Toby's. Riley knocked and waited for Toby to answer the door. Toby was like a grandparent to all the kids on the block.

"Riley! Hello!" she said when she opened the door. "Are you here with your Mama today?"

"Hi, Toby," replied Riley. "Mama had to cover someone's shift at the library today. She says hi. These are my friends, Lea and Cricket."

Toby had a big smile, and Lea and Cricket couldn't help smiling back. Toby opened the door wide.

"Come on in," she said.

The three friends stepped into Toby's hall and looked around.

"We've brought you daffodil bulbs," said Riley.

"Well, that's awfully kind. You can leave the bulbs right here in the hall," Toby said.

"Oh, and Mama sent a new library book for you. She thought you might like this one," Riley said.

Riley and Toby looked over every detail on the cover. The cover had a teenage girl with long hair and a serious face. She was wearing a suit of armor and holding a sword up high. Behind her a big green dragon breathed fire.

"This looks like fun. I'll tell you the whole story when I'm done," Toby said.

Riley smiled, "I can't wait!"

Riley didn't read books that long yet, but Toby told the stories just right. Toby liked books with dragons and swords on the cover, or crowns and castles, or sometimes a planet or a spaceship.

Some of Toby's books looked just like Dad's paintings. In fact, Dad did the cover art for one of Toby's favorite series. Riley loved giving Toby updates about it.

Riley said, "You know, Dad's working on the cover for the next Throne of Flame and Truth book."

Toby's eyes went wide. "I can't wait!"

Riley took the book through to Toby's special reading chair. It was right by the window with a view of the park across the street. They added the new book to the tall "to read" stack. It wobbled like a Jenga tower.

"Psst, Riley?" whispered Cricket. "Can you ask Toby for a snack?"

"What? Why?" Riley whispered back. "We just had lunch at my place."

"Most of my lunch went into the Jenga tower!" whispered Cricket.

Riley huffed a little. "Why don't you ask her?"

"I don't know her as well as you do. I don't want to be rude," Cricket said.

"Fine," Riley replied.

Riley braced to ask Toby if they could have a snack but needn't have bothered. Toby called Riley and Cricket into the kitchen, where Lea was eating Rice Krispie treats.

"Come eat, kids," said Toby, smiling wide. "I bet you're hungry."

She didn't have to tell Cricket twice. He practically leaped at the treats. Toby gave them a juice box and let Cricket take two treats in his pocket for later.

"Thanks, Toby," said Cricket. "These are the best Rice Krispie treats I have ever had!"

"You're welcome, honey. Anytime," said Toby as she smiled even wider.

CHAPTER THREE

WHAT'S IN A NAME?

Toby waved them off from her front door. Riley, Cricket, and Lea took the short walk across Wilder Street to the park.

"Huh," said Cricket. "The park has a name."

"Yeah," said Riley. "The Wilder Street Park."

"No, look. There's a plaque. I guess I've

never come to the park from this direction before," Cricket said. "The Hernández Family Community Park."

"I wonder who the Hernándezes are," said Riley the moment before the three friends ran into the park.

Riley, Cricket, and Lea kicked Lea's soccer ball around for a while. Lea always carried her ball in a sack. She was never without it.

"How do you get a park named after you?" wondered Cricket.

Riley and Lea looked around the park. There was blacktop by the patchy field of grass where they stood. On the blacktop some older kids played four square. Lea was nervous around older kids, so she looked away.

"Maybe they were a famous soccer family," said Riley, kicking the soccer ball to Lea. Or *near* Lea—Riley was still working on their soccer game.

Riley started commentating the game as Lea practiced a fake-out move she was trying to get the hang of. "Reynolds passes to Crane, who does a spectacular move to get the ball past Hernández."

Cricket laughed and ran down the pitch. Riley kept going. "Parker gets into position to receive the ball, dodging the other Hernández at every step."

Cricket dashed to where he thought "position" might be. Lea pushed the ball smoothly forward to Cricket.

"Parker receives the pass. Yet another Hernández is all over him! Hernández tries to steal the ball! Parker passes to Crane, left wide open by the Hernándezes! Crane shoots . . ." Lea kicked the ball at a tree, hitting it right in the trunk with a *THUNK*.

Riley kept announcing. ". . . And scores! South Philly wins the World Cup against the Hernández family! What an upset! The scrappy underdogs win against the best soccer-playing family in the world! I can't believe it!"

Lea, Cricket, and Riley paraded and celebrated, waving to the cheering crowds of imaginary fans. They flopped onto the grass laughing.

"I think the Hernández family made wildlife documentaries," said Cricket after a moment.

He flipped onto his stomach and pretended to hold a camera up to his eye, filming the squirrels hopping between branches and bounding across the grass. He used that special voice that documentary narrators have. "This is the first footage ever captured of the rare and dangerous gray squirrel in its native habitat."

Riley laughed and pulled out their own pretend camera. "The gray squirrel can spit venom up to fifty feet. It takes just *seconds* to kill an adult elephant."

Lea toed the soccer ball and said, "I read about a frog that could do that. It lives in Costa Rica. But it doesn't spit venom. You have to lick it to get poisoned."

"Don't lick a gray squirrel, either. They are more deadly to humans than a crocodile and a hippopotamus combined," Cricket said in his narrator's voice.

"A crocopotamus?" asked Lea.

"Huh?" asked Cricket in his regular voice.

"You said a crocodile and a hippopotamus combined," Lea laughed.

"Ha!" laughed Cricket. "Maybe that's a new species that the Hernández family discovered!"

A loud yell came from the older kids on the blacktop. One of them was shouting and waving his arms around. That older kid seemed really mad about something.

CHAPTER FOUR

FANCY PARKS AND MEMORIES

Lea lay lower in the grass. Taking Lea's lead, Riley and Cricket lay low in the grass too. They pretended that they were special agents spying on the older kids. But a game of being sneaky gets boring quickly if the people you're sneaking on don't know they're being sneaked on.

Riley picked up an acorn and threw it at Lea's soccer ball. It pinged off the ball in a surprising direction, and a new game was born. They threw acorns, trying to hit the ball and predict which direction the acorn would ping away. It was a nice day to be outside, but there wasn't much to do at the Hernández Family Community Park—even if you used your imagination.

"What's your favorite park, Lea?" asked Riley.

"Lenape, of course." Lenape Park is where Lea had junior league soccer matches and practices. This season she was the captain of the Zephyrs. "That summer it was closed was the worst."

"Yeah," said Cricket, "that was a looooong summer." He threw an acorn that pinged straight upward. "Did you see that?"

"Nice!" said Lea. "That whole summer the Zephyrs had to go three neighborhoods over for matches. We had to practice on a baseball field."

"But," said Riley, throwing an acorn and missing the ball completely, "that summer we figured out how good your street is for kicking a ball around." Lea lived in a row house on a narrow, dead-end street a few blocks from Riley. No cars ever went up there.

"That was awesome," Lea agreed. "But when Lenape reopened? That soccer pitch was perfect. So green and flat. There were no dusty patches or uneven parts. It really upped the Zephyrs' game."

"But they took away the swing sets," said Cricket, taking the slightly squashed Rice Krispie treats out of his pocket and dividing them up to share. "I like any park with swings."

"This park has swings," said Lea, standing up.

Trying not to call the attention of the older kids, the friends crossed the park to the blacktop and the swings. They climbed on and tried to swing so high they turned upside down.

"This park would be better with a dog run," said Lea.

"At the park by my mom's place you can see the dog run from the swings. That's my favorite park," Cricket said. "It's awesome."

Riley didn't say what their favorite park was. They didn't know how to say what was so special about it. It wasn't that good of a park. It was small, mostly paved, with no swings or dog runs.

But it was where Dad had been taking Riley since they were a baby. It was called Welcome Park, and it was halfway between Riley's house and the library where Mama worked.

It all started one day when baby Riley was being fussy, refusing to take an afternoon nap. Dad—with frazzled hair, of course—strapped Riley into a baby carrier and started walking. Riley fell asleep and Dad and Mama met at Welcome Park. They discovered the taco place right across the street and started a new family tradition.

For Riley's whole life, they had eaten tacos at Welcome Park at least once a week. Now it wasn't when Riley wouldn't take a nap. It was days when the weather was nice, and Dad couldn't face cooking dinner.

"What this park needs," said Riley, arcing high on the swings, "is tacos."

Lea laughed, jumping off her swing. "Every park needs tacos!"

She kicked her soccer ball at the tetherball pole. It rebounded—right toward the bigger kids.

CHAPTER FIVE

SIX KIDS, FOUR SQUARES

The soccer ball rolled across the blacktop, headed right for the kids playing four square. Riley held their breath, Lea squealed, and Cricket gasped.

The biggest kid, the one who had been yelling before, stopped Lea's ball with his foot. He picked it up, held it high, and shouted, "Hey! Is this yours?"

Lea squealed again. By the time Riley and Cricket climbed off the swings, the big kid had walked over and was handing the ball back to Lea. "I saw you kicking around before. You're pretty good."

"Uh," Lea stammered. "Uh, thanks."

"Sure," said the older kid. "Leon has to go home and three square is boring. You wanna play? I'm Luca."

"Uh, I'm Lea. This is Riley and Cricket," Lea said. She looked at Riley and Cricket, eyes wide, asking silently what she should do. Riley linked an arm through Lea's and smiled wide at Luca.

"Sure, Luca. That sounds fun."

On the chalked-up four square grid, Luca introduced two other kids—Xavvy and Juana.

Xavvy's face lit up. "Oh, hey! You were the knight and dragon group costume on dress-up day at school, right?"

"Right!" said Riley.

Xavvy held up a hand for a high five. "That costume was epic." When Lea got her high five from Xavvy, her face split into a grin.

"I was the knight," said Lea.

"Right on," Xavvy replied.

"What did you go as?" asked Riley.

Xavvy rolled his eyes. "One of a million Captain Underpantses. I gotta step it up next year."

"Have you played four square before?" asked Luca, bouncing the ball. The three friends all shook their heads. "It's easy enough to learn."

"Easy to learn," added Juana, grinning, "but hard to master."

"Those are the best kind of games," said Lea.

"For sure they are!" agreed Riley.

In no time, Lea, Cricket, and Riley got the rules of the game. They learned about house rules with names like Black Captain, Cherry Bomb, Bus Stop, and Passback. They learned that you could make up rules as you go along—the sillier the better. They learned that when Luca had been yelling before, it was because there was a rule called Tyrant Ball that basically just meant he had to shout at everyone the whole time. He wasn't actually mad. Then they learned that the squares were called Peasant, Duke, Prince, and King.

"We can do better than that, right?" asked Riley. They quickly settled on Acorn, Sapling, Tree, and Forest. And the game began.

Luca was good at the game, and no one could topple him from the Forest square. Except Lea. Riley never got past Acorn, but they didn't mind. It was as much fun to watch as it was to play—cheering along, chasing down the ball when it went out of bounds, and trying to distract Luca so he'd miss a shot. And making up new rules, of course.

Riley and Cricket were really good at making up rules. Alphabetical Fruit, No Such Thing as Out of Bounds, Two Square Sudden Death, Cutest French Bulldog on the Block, and more. Lea, Xavvy, Juana, and Luca laughed and tumbled around on the blacktop, trying to keep up with plays that Riley and Cricket called from the sidelines. And it turned out that Lea was even better at Tyrant Ball than Luca!

After playing a while, Riley stood on the sidelines with Juana. Riley's phone beeped with a text from Dad.

I finished the painting! I think it turned out okay!

YAY! Riley replied.

Just cleaning up. You still at the park? asked Dad.

Yup, replied Riley. *We're playing with some new friends.*

Fun! replied Dad. *I'll bring supper to the park. Lea's and Cricket's families are coming too. Cookout!*

Riley replied with a string of excited emojis. At the next game break, Riley told Lea and Cricket the plan for supper.

"Cool!" said Juana from the Acorn square.

"We can play all night!" added Lea from Forest.

Riley turned to Xavvy, who was on the sidelines, and asked, "Did you know this park has a name?"

"Of course!" said Xavvy. "It's the Hernández Family Community Park."

"I never knew that. We were trying to figure out who the Hernández family might be," Riley said.

Xavvy smiled. "I might have an idea," he said.

Before he could say more, Toby called to the kids from her stoop. She had more Rice Krispie treats and juice boxes and . . . a shovel?

"Hernández kids!" she called. "Come have a snack. Then I've got a job for you."

Luca, Xavvy, and Juana yelled back, "Coming, Grandma Hernández!"

"You can come too," said Luca.

"We're in!" said Cricket. Who said no to more of Toby's Rice Krispie treats?

"Wait!" said Riley. "You're the Hernández family?"

"Yup!" the three Hernándezes whooped, dashing across Wilder Street to Toby's stoop. Riley, Lea, and Cricket followed.

CHAPTER SIX

A COMMUNITY PARK, FOR REAL

"You own the park?" asked Lea.

"Not quite," laughed Toby. "The park was named for my tata and abuela."

"Wow," said Cricket, taking a treat in each hand. "What'd they do to get a park named after them? Were they rich?"

"They were not rich, but they worked hard," Toby said. "Abuela did hair, and Tata delivered mail."

"So, how did they get a park?" asked Cricket.

"They loved their family and their community," said Toby. "It's that simple."

"But plenty of people love their families and don't get a park named after them," said Lea.

"Ah," said Toby. "That's true, isn't it. Well, I guess Abuela and Tata loved in a big way. They volunteered a lot. They never turned away anyone hungry or cold or lost. And back then, there were a lot of people like that in this neighborhood. Abuela did everyone's hair—didn't matter who, didn't matter if they could pay. And

Tata coached Little League for forty years or more. Best coach I ever had!"

"Cool," Riley said. "And now the park is named for you all too since you're the Hernández family?"

Toby nodded. "They're big shoes to fill, but we do what we can to be of service to others, right, mis corazónes?"

Luca, Xavvy, and Juana nodded. "Tata and Abuela would be very proud of you." Toby said as she hugged her grandkids tight and gave them each a big sloppy kiss. All four Hernándezes beamed.

Soon, the Rice Krispie treats were gone and the juice boxes were empty. Everyone had a new burst of energy.

"Luca, run next door and ask to borrow Mr. Eddie's trowel."

"Sure, Grandma," said Luca, and he left to ring the doorbell next door.

"And come on, the rest of you," said Toby. "Grab a shovel or a tote bag." They were the same tote bags that Riley, Lea, and Cricket had carried to Toby's earlier.

"The daffodils?" asked Riley. "What're we doing with these?"

"Giving the community and the park some love," replied Toby with a wink.

They all walked back across Wilder Street to the Hernández Family Community Park. Luca joined them with Mr. Eddie's trowel. Together they planted every last one of the daffodil bulbs. There were hundreds. But with so many hands in the dirt, it took no time at all. Riley loved the feeling of having their hands deep in the ground.

Lea made sure her daffodils were in perfectly straight lines. Cricket made sure his bulbs spelled code that only he could read. Riley made sure to give each bulb they planted a little bit of extra love. They wanted anybody who saw them bloom next spring to know that they were welcome in the Hernández Family Community Park.

The kids finished planting, washed up, and returned Mr. Eddie's trowel. The shadows were long, and the afternoon was nearly over.

Just then Riley's dad arrived at the park with his portable grill and a backpack full of hot dogs and buns. He fired up the coals. Riley introduced their dad to their new friends.

As Riley's dad talked to Toby, the kids went back to playing four square until the street lights came on. Riley made up four new rules.

Soon enough, Cricket's parents arrived in their minivan with Cricket's little half-brothers and -sisters. They popped the back hatch and brought out blankets, folding chairs, and coolers full of fresh lemonade, coleslaw, and fruit salad. During the summer the Parkers were always ready for outdoor adventures.

"Then Lea's mom arrived with her marinated zucchini (which went straight onto Riley's dad's grill), her corn fritters (which went straight into Riley's dad's mouth), and Lea's older sister (who barely looked up from her phone).

The Hernándezes fired up the grill Toby kept on the sidewalk in front of her house, sending plumes of juicy burger smell all over the block.

Mr. Eddie was invited from his stoop to sit in one of the Parkers' folding chairs. Mr. Parker handed him a glass of lemonade and a toddler to fuss over. Riley's mama arrived straight from work. Riley told her all about the day's games and excitement.

Then more people from around the neighborhood arrived with their picnics or portable grills. Everyone brought a little something, and everyone was fed until they were full.

As the pink-orange sunset dissolved from the sky and a few stars came out, someone brought out a guitar and someone else had a harmonica. A neighborhood band! Riley wanted to join in. They looked around for something to drum on. Ah-ha!

"Mrs. Parker? May I borrow your coleslaw container?" asked Riley.

Mrs. Parker said, "It's all yours, honey!"

Riley wiped out the container and turned it upside down. They gave it a little tap. It sounded good enough for a makeshift drum.

They sat on the grass between the guitar, the harmonica, and another guitar someone had run home to get. They drummed along, feeling the beat of the park. It was the beat of a loving neighborhood.

The whole park lit up with laughing and singing and dancing. The Hernández Family Community Park might not have had tacos, a soccer pitch, a dog run, or the best swings, but it had heart. And that made it extra special.

THE END

DISCUSSION QUESTIONS

1. When they are bored at the park, Riley and their friends use their imaginations. Why is it important to be creative and use your imagination?

2. When your friends have different ideas of how to play, how does that make you feel? What do you do?

3. The Hernández family had a park named after them. If you could name a park after someone, who would it be and why?

WRITING PROMPTS

1. Riley and their parents have a special tradition of having tacos in the park. Write about a special tradition you have with your family or friends.

2. One of Riley's favorite places is Welcome Park. Write about your favorite place. Include a drawing as well.

3. Playing video games and watching TV are fun, but it's important to get outside and play as well. Make a list of at least five reasons you need to go outside every day.

MEET THE CREATORS

Jay Albee is the pen name for an LGBTQ+ couple named Jen Breach and J. Anthony. Between them they've done lots of jobs: archaeologist, illustrator, ticket taker, and bagel baker, but now they write and draw all day long in their row house in South Philadelphia, Pennsylvania.

Jen's favorite park has a big slope perfect for rolling down again and again. J. loves any park with dogs, swings, or a taco truck.

Jen Breach

J. Anthony